THE WISEST ANSWER

Written By David R. Collins

Illustrated By Deborah G. Wilson

Milliken Publishing Company, St. Louis, Missouri

To Fred and Pat,
with a tip of the hat!

D.R.C.

To my daughter, Aubra.

D.G.W.

Series Editors: Patricia and Fredrick McKissack
Cover Design by Graphcom, Inc., St. Louis, Missouri
Logo Design by Justmann Associates, St. Louis, Missouri

Library of Congress Catalog Card Number: 87-61640
ISBN 0-88335-751-8 / ISBN 0-88335-731-3 (lib. bdg.)

For weeks the forest animals had been waiting.
Now the big day had come.
Three young owlets were about to be tested.

"Ollie, Lillie, and Millie, listen closely," said Old Owl. "Our forest friends will ask you questions. You must try to give your wisest answers."

Ollie and Lillie smiled.
But Millie did not smile.
She was frightened.
She did not feel wise at all.
She still liked to play.

Old Owl blinked her eyes.
"We will now begin the test," she said.
"Do your very best."

Young Mouse asked Ollie the first question.
"Which is the most important —
food, clothing, or shelter?"

"Food is most important," said Ollie
"The big mountain lion hunts.
So does the small ant.
Without food you and your family would not live.
What good would clothing or shelter be then?"

"I will tell the other mice what you have said," said Young Mouse, running into the bushes. Old Owl watched and listened.

Seeing Hawk sat on a tree limb.
“Lillie, how far is far?” he asked.

Lillie was ready with an answer.
"Far is from here to there.
And when you get there,
far has moved to another there."

The forest animals cheered.
“Your answer is interesting,” said Seeing Hawk.
Old Owl said nothing.
She watched and listened.

Next, Big Bear and Fast Squirrel
came out of the bushes.
"Millie, which is more important —
speed or strength?" they asked.
Big Bear growled,
"I think it is strength."

“Tell him it is speed,” Fast Squirrel said to Millie.
“Yes indeed! Yes indeed!”

Millie didn't know what to say.
She had studied, but she didn't have an answer.
"I don't know," Millie said.

"See, I told you I was right," said Fast Squirrel.
"No, I was right," said Big Bear.
Ollie laughed. Lillie did too.
Soon many of the forest animals were laughing.
Old Owl blinked, but she said nothing.
Millie felt foolish.

Slow Turtle slid forward.
"How much is many? How little is few?"

Ollie answered quickly.
"Many is more than just a few.
And a few is not as many as much."

"Sounds wise to me," said Slow Turtle, tipping his shell.

Proud Peacock spoke next.
“Which color is the most beautiful?”
“The rainbow!” said Lillie.
“All the colors make one beautiful sight.”

“I like your answer,” said Proud Peacock.

Quick Deer turned to Millie and asked
"How many raindrops are
there in a shower?"
Millie thought and thought.
No answer came to her.
"I don't know," she said.

Quick Deer looked at Old Owl.
Old Owl blinked and watched and listened.
Poor Millie. She wanted to cry.

But Old Owl spoke.
"Millie, answer these questions as best you can."
Millie was never more frightened.
She listened carefully.

"How many soap bubbles are in a bar of soap?" Old Owl asked.
"I—I don't know," Millie answered.
"Which is strongest — fire, wind, or water?"
"I don't know."
"Is summer better than winter?
Is day better than night?"

“I don’t know! I don’t know!” cried Millie.

Ollie and Lillie laughed.
Millie was very ashamed.
She flew away and cried.

Later that night, when the moon was bright,
Millie heard her friends calling,
"Millie! Millie!"
It was Ollie and Lillie.
Millie did not want to answer,
but she did.

"We are sorry for laughing at your answers,"
said Ollie. "Please come back.
Old Owl said your answers were the best."

Millie shook her head.
She did not understand.
Lillie said, “Our answers only sounded good.
They made the forest animals feel good.”

"But I didn't answer any of the
questions," said Millie.
"That's just it," said Ollie.
"Old Owl said that when you don't know the answer,
'I don't know'
is the wisest answer of all."

Vocabulary

a
about
all
an
and
animals
another
answer(s)
answered
ant
any
are
as
ashamed
ask
asked
at
away
back
bar
be
beautiful
been
begin
best
better
big
Big Bear
blinked
bright
bubbles
bushes
but
by
calling
came
can
carefully
cheered
closely
clothing
color(s)
come
cried
cry
day
did
didn't
do
does
don't
eyes
family
far
Fast Squirrel
feel
felt
few
fire
first
flew
food
foolish
for
forest
forward
friends
frightened
from
get
give
good
growled
had
has
have
he
head
heard
her
here
him
his
how
hunts
I
important
in
indeed
interesting
into
is
it
just
know
later
laughed
laughing
like
liked
Lillie
limb
lion
listen
listened
little
live
looked
made
make
many
me
mice
Millie
moon
more
most
mountain
mouse
moved
much
must
never
next
night
no
not
nothing
now
of
Old Owl
Ollie
on
one
or
other
our
out
owlets
play
please
poor
Proud Peacock
question(s)
Quick Deer
quickly
rainbow
raindrops
ready
right
running
said
sat
say
see
Seeing Hawk
she
shell
shelter
shook
shower
sight
slid
Slow Turtle
small
smile
smiled
so
soap
soon
sorry
sounded
sounds
speed
spoke
still
strength
strongest
studied
summer
tell
test
tested
than
that
the
then
there
these
they
think
thought
three
tipping
to
told
too
tree
try
turned
understand
very
waited
waiting
want
wanted
was
watched
water
we
weeks
were
what
when
which
will
wind
winter
wise
wisest
with
without
would
yes
you
young
Young Mouse
your